How Zebras Got Their Stripes

A tale from Africa

Retold by Lesley Sims

Illustrated by Laure Fournier

This story is about

a greedy
baboon,

a pond,

a giraffe,

an elephant

and the
very first
zebra.

Long ago, there was a greedy baboon.

He lived by a pond.

He wanted the pond all
to himself.

Everyone was thirsty.

Baboon didn't care.

7

Giraffe crept to
the pond.

Baboon **roared**.
He waved his arms and
jumped up and down.

Giraffe fled.

Elephant went to the pond.

Baboon **roared**. He jumped up and down and waved his arms.

Elephant fled.

Zebra walked up.

Baboon **roared**.
Zebra stamped his hoof.

"It's not your pond,"
he said. "You must
share it."

"No!" said Baboon.
"Go away."

Baboon got lots of sticks.

He piled them by
the pond.

Zebra wasn't scared.

18

He ran at Baboon.

He kicked out his legs.

Baboon flew into the air.

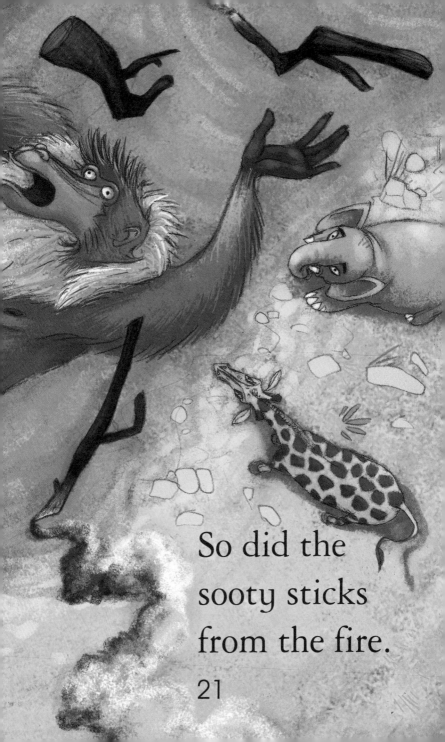

So did the
sooty sticks
from the fire.

21

The sticks landed
on Zebra.

Baboon landed on his bottom.

Ever since then, zebras
have had black stripes.

And baboons have had
red bottoms.

PUZZLES

Puzzle 1
Put the pictures in order.

A

B

C

D

E

F

Puzzle 2

A

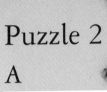

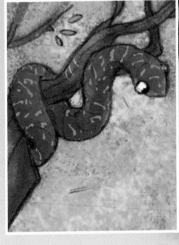

B

C

Can you spot
the mistake in
each picture?

Puzzle 3
Choose the best sentence.

A

Giraffe has spots!

Giraffe has stripes!

B

Baboon is greedy!

Baboon is green!

Puzzle 4
Can you find these things in the picture?

Elephant	Giraffe	pond
Zebra	Baboon	tail
bananas	trunk	

Answers to puzzles

Puzzle 1

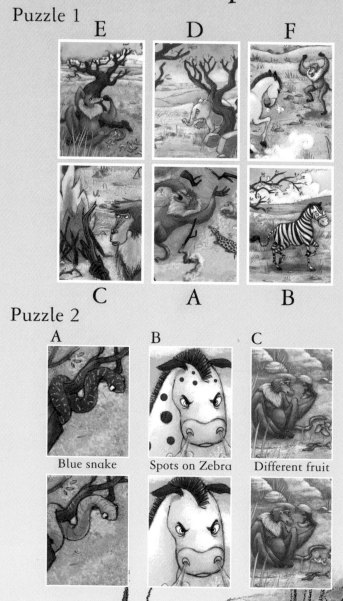

E D F

C A B

Puzzle 2

A B C

Blue snake Spots on Zebra Different fruit

Puzzle 3

A — Giraffe has spots!

B — Baboon is greedy!

Puzzle 4

Giraffe

bananas

Zebra   Elephant

trunk

tail   Baboon   pond

About the story

This story is based on an old folktale from Namibia in Africa.

Designed by Nancy Leschnikoff
Additional design by Emily Bornoff
Series designer: Russell Punter

First published in 2009 by Usborne Publishing Ltd., Usborne House,
83-85 Saffron Hill, London EC1N 8RT, England. www.usborne.com
Copyright © 2009 Usborne Publishing Ltd.